THE CHRISTMAS MIRACLE ~OF~ JONATHAN TOOMEY

The Christmas Miracle  of Jonathan Toomey

Susan Wojciechowski

ILLUSTRATED BY

P. J. Lynch

WALKER BOOKS
AND SUBSIDIARIES

LONDON · BOSTON · SYDNEY · AUCKLAND

For Joel, with love

S.W.

For Fran and Wordy

*With special thanks to
Nicole and Nicholas and Jack
and the Shelburne Museum, Vermont*

P.J.L.

THE VILLAGE CHILDREN
CALLED HIM MR GLOOMY.

But, in fact, his name was Toomey, Mr Jonathan Toomey. And though it's not kind to call people names, this one fitted quite well. For Jonathan Toomey seldom smiled and never laughed. He went about mumbling and grumbling, muttering and sputtering, grumping and griping. He complained that the church bells rang too often, that the birds sang too shrilly, that the children played too loudly.

Mr Toomey was a wood-carver. Some said he was the best wood-carver in the whole valley. He spent his days sitting at a workbench, carving beautiful shapes from blocks of pine and hickory and chestnut wood. After supper, he sat in a straight-backed chair near the fireplace, smoking his pipe and staring into the flames.

Jonathan Toomey wasn't an old man, but if you saw him, you might think he was, the way he walked bent forwards with his head down. You wouldn't notice his eyes, the clear blue of an August sky. And you wouldn't see the dimple on his chin, since his face was mostly hidden under a shaggy, untrimmed beard, speckled with sawdust and wood shavings and, depending on what he'd eaten that day, crumbs of bread or a bit of potato or dried gravy.

The village people didn't know it, but there was a reason for his gloom, a reason for his grumbling, a reason why he walked hunched over, as if carrying a great weight on his shoulders. Some years earlier, when Jonathan Toomey was young and full of life and full of love, his wife and baby had become very ill. And, because those were the days before hospitals and medicines and skilled doctors, his wife and baby had died, three days apart from each other.

So Jonathan Toomey had packed his belongings into a wagon and travelled till his tears stopped. He settled into a tiny house at the edge of a village to do his wood-carving.

One day in early December, there was a knock at Jonathan's door. Mumbling and grumbling, he went to answer it. There stood a woman and a young boy.

"I'm the widow McDowell. I'm new to your village. This is my son, Thomas," the woman said.

"I'm seven and I know how to whistle," said Thomas.

"Whistling is pish-posh," said the wood-carver gruffly.

"I need something carved," said the woman and she told Jonathan about a very special set of Christmas figures her grandfather had carved for her when she was a girl.

"After I moved here, I discovered that they were lost," she explained. "I had hoped that by some miracle I would find them again, but it hasn't happened."

"There are no such things as miracles," the wood-carver told her. "Now, could you describe the figures for me?"

"There were sheep," she told him.

"Two of them, with curly wool," added Thomas.

"Yes, two," said the widow, "and a cow, an angel, Mary, Joseph, the Baby Jesus, and the Wise Men."

"Three of them," added Thomas.

"Will you take the job?" asked the widow McDowell.

"I will."

"I'm grateful. How soon can you have them ready?"

"They will be ready when they are ready," he said.

"But I must have them by Christmas. They mean very much to me. I can't remember a Christmas without them."

"Christmas is pish-posh," said Jonathan gruffly and he shut the door.

The following week there was a knock at the wood-carver's door. Muttering and sputtering, he went to answer it. There stood the widow McDowell and Thomas.

"Excuse me," said the widow, "but Thomas has been begging to come and watch you work. He says he wants to be a wood-carver when he grows up and would like to watch you since you are the best in the valley."

"I'll be quiet. You won't even know I'm here. Please, please," piped in Thomas.

With a grumble, the wood-carver stepped aside to let them in. He pointed to a stool near his workbench. "No talking, no jiggling, no noise," he ordered Thomas.

The widow McDowell handed Mr Toomey a warm loaf of corn bread as a token of thanks. Then she took out her knitting and sat down in a rocking-chair in the far corner of the cottage.

"Not there!" bellowed the wood-carver. "No one sits in that chair." So she moved to the straight-backed chair by the fire.

Thomas sat very still. Once, when he needed to sneeze, he pressed a finger under his nose to hold it back. Once, when he wanted desperately to scratch his leg, he counted to twenty to keep his mind off the itch.

After a very long time, Thomas cleared his throat and whispered, "Mr Toomey, may I ask a question?"

The wood-carver glared at Thomas, then shrugged his shoulders and grunted. Thomas decided it meant "yes", so he went on. "Is that my sheep you're carving?"

The wood-carver nodded and grunted again.

After another very long time, Thomas whispered, "Mr Toomey, excuse me, but you're carving my sheep wrong."

The widow McDowell's knitting-needles stopped clicking. Jonathan Toomey's knife stopped carving. Thomas went on. "It's a beautiful sheep, nice and curly, but my sheep looked happy."

"That's pish-posh," said Mr Toomey. "Sheep are sheep. They cannot look happy."

"Mine did," said Thomas. "They knew they were with the Baby Jesus, so they were happy."

After that, Thomas was quiet for the rest of the afternoon. When the church bells chimed six o'clock, Mr Toomey grumbled under his breath about the awful noise. The widow McDowell said it was time to leave. Thomas sneezed three times, then thanked the wood-carver for allowing him to watch.

That evening, after a supper of corn bread and boiled potatoes, the wood-carver sat down at his bench. He picked up his knife. He picked up the sheep. He worked until his eyelids drooped shut.

A few days later there was a knock at the wood-carver's door. Griping and grumbling, he went to answer it. There stood the widow and her son.

"May I watch again? I will be quiet," said Thomas.

He settled himself on the stool very quietly, while his mother laid a basket of sweet-smelling raisin buns on the table.

"The teapot is warm," Mr Toomey said gruffly, his head bent over his work.

While Mr Toomey carved, the widow McDowell poured tea. She touched the wood-carver gently on the shoulder and placed a cup of tea and a bun next to him. He pretended not to notice, but soon, both the plate and the cup were empty.

Thomas tried to eat the bun his mother had given him as quietly as he could. But it is almost impossible to be seven and eat a warm sticky raisin bun without making various smacking, licking, satisfied noises.

When Thomas had finished, he tried to sit quietly. Once, he almost hiccupped, but he took a deep breath and held it till his face turned red. And once, without thinking, he began to swing his legs, but a glare from the wood-carver stopped him and he kept them so still they fell asleep.

After a very long time, Thomas whispered, "Mr Toomey, excuse me, may I ask a question?"

Grunt.

"Is that my cow you're carving?"

Nod and grunt.

Another very long time went by. Then Thomas cleared his throat and said, "Mr Toomey, excuse me, but I must tell you something. That is a beautiful cow, the most beautiful cow I have ever seen, but it's not right. My cow looked proud."

"That's pish-posh," growled the wood-carver. "Cows are cows. They cannot look proud."

"My cow did. It knew that Jesus chose to be born in its barn, so it was proud."

Thomas was quiet for the rest of the afternoon. The only sounds that could be heard were the scraping of the carving knife, the humming of the widow McDowell and the *click-click* of her knitting-needles.

When the church bells chimed six o'clock, Mr Toomey muttered under his breath about the noise. The widow McDowell said it was time to leave. Thomas shook first one leg, then the other. He thanked the wood-carver for allowing him to watch.

That evening, after a supper of boiled potatoes and raisin buns, the wood-carver sat down at his bench. He picked up his carving knife. He picked up the cow. He worked until his eyelids drooped shut.

A few days later there was a knock on the wood-carver's door. He smoothed down his hair as he went to answer it. At the door were the widow and her son.

"May I watch again?" asked Thomas.

As Mrs McDowell warmed the tea and put a plate of fresh molasses biscuits on the workbench, Thomas watched the wood-carver work on the figure of an angel.

After a very long time, Thomas spoke. "Mr Toomey, excuse me, is that my angel you're carving?"

"Yes. And would you do me the favour of telling me exactly what I'm doing wrong?"

"Well, my angel looked like one of God's most important angels, because it was sent to Baby Jesus."

"And just how does one make an angel look important?" asked the wood-carver.

"You'll be able to do it," said Thomas. "You are the best wood-carver in the valley."

After another very long time, Thomas spoke. "Mr Toomey, excuse me, may I ask a question?"

"Do you ever stop talking?" asked the wood-carver.

"My mother says I don't. She says I could learn about the virtue of silence from you."

Under his beard, the wood-carver's face turned pink. The widow McDowell's face turned as red as the scarf she was knitting.

"Well, speak up, what is your question?"

"Will you please teach me to carve?"

"I am a very busy man," grumbled the wood-carver. But he put down the important angel. "You will carve a bird."

"A robin, I hope," said Thomas. "I like robins."

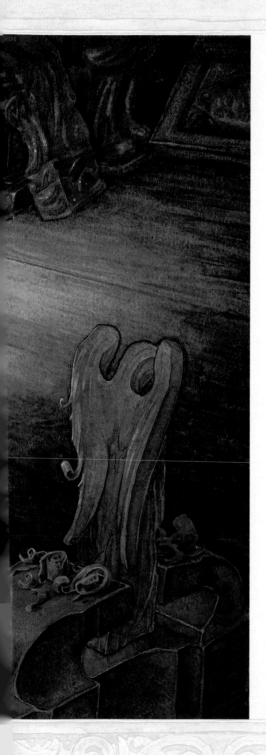

With a piece of charcoal, the wood-carver sketched a robin on a piece of brown paper. He handed Thomas a small block of pine and a knife. He showed him how to lop the corners from the block and slowly smooth the edges of the wood into curves.

Thomas copied the wood-carver's strokes, head bent, tongue working from side to side of his lower lip as he concentrated.

When the church bells chimed six o'clock, Jonathan Toomey was holding Thomas' hand in his, guiding the knife along the edge of a wing. He didn't hear them ringing. The widow McDowell said it was time to leave. Thomas brushed wood shavings from his shirt. Then he reached out and brushed two especially large pieces of wood shaving from Jonathan Toomey's beard. He thanked the wood-carver for teaching him how to carve.

Later, after a supper of boiled potatoes and molasses biscuits, Jonathan Toomey went to his workbench. He thought for a long time. He sketched drawing after drawing. Finally, he picked up his carving knife. He picked up the angel. He carved until his eyelids drooped shut.

A few days later, there was a knock on the wood-carver's door. Mr Toomey jumped up to answer it.

There stood the widow McDowell with a bouquet of pine branches and holly sprigs, dotted with berries. And there stood Thomas, clutching his partly-carved robin.

While Thomas and Mr Toomey carved, Mrs McDowell put the branches in a jar of water. She scrubbed Mr Toomey's kitchen table and set the jar in the centre, on a pretty cloth embroidered with lilies of the valley and daisies which she found in a drawer below the cupboard.

"Next, I will carve the Wise Men and Joseph," the wood-carver said to Thomas. "Perhaps, before I begin, you will tell me about the mistakes I am going to make."

"Well," said Thomas, "my Wise Men were wearing their most wonderful robes because they were going to visit Jesus, and my Joseph was leaning over Baby Jesus like he was protecting him. He looked very serious."

It wasn't until the church bells had chimed and the widow and her son were preparing to go that Mr Toomey saw the jar of pine branches and the scrubbed table and the cloth embroidered with lilies of the valley and daisies.

"I found the cloth in a drawer. I thought it would look pretty on the table," the widow McDowell said, smiling.

"Never open that drawer," the wood-carver said harshly.

When the two had left, Jonathan put the cloth away.

That evening, after a supper of boiled potatoes, the wood-carver worked on Joseph and the Wise Men until his eyelids drooped shut.

A few days later there was a knock on the wood-carver's door. He dusted the crumbs from his beard and brushed the sawdust from his shirt. At the door were the widow McDowell and Thomas.

All afternoon Thomas watched the wood-carver work. When it was time to leave, Jonathan said to Thomas, "I am about to begin the last two figures – Mary and the baby. Can you tell me how your figures looked?"

"They were the most special of all," said Thomas. "Jesus was smiling and reaching up to his mother and Mary looked like she loved him very much."

"Thank you, Thomas," said the wood-carver.

"Tomorrow is Christmas. Is there any chance the figures will be ready?" the widow McDowell asked.

"They will be ready when they are ready."

"I understand," said the widow, and she handed Jonathan two parcels. "Merry Christmas," she said.

Jonathan folded his arms across his chest. "I want no presents," he said harshly.

"That is exactly why we are giving them," answered the widow. She put them down on the table and left.

Jonathan sat down at the table. Slowly, he opened the first parcel. Inside was a red scarf, hand-knitted, warm and bright. He tied the scarf around his neck.

The other parcel held a robin, crudely carved of pine. A smile twitched at the corners of Jonathan's mouth as he ran his fingers over the lopsided wings. He dusted the mantelpiece with his sleeve and placed the robin exactly in the centre, so he could look at it from his chair.

The wood-carver did not eat supper that day. Instead he began to sketch the final figures, Mary and Jesus. He drew Mary, then crumpled the sketch into a ball and tossed it on the floor. He drew the baby, crumpled the sketch into a ball and tossed it with the first. He sketched again. Once more he crumpled the paper. Soon there was a small mountain of crumpled papers at his feet. He picked up a block of wood and tried to carve, but his knife would not do what he wanted it to do. He hurled the chunk of wood into the fireplace and sat, staring into the flames.

When he heard the church bells announcing the midnight Christmas service, he got up. Slowly he opened the drawer beneath the cupboard, the drawer he had told the widow never to open.

From it he took the cloth embroidered with lilies of the valley and daisies. He took out a rough woollen shawl and a lace handkerchief. He took out a tiny white baby blanket and a little pair of blue socks. He placed each piece gently on the floor. From the bottom of the drawer he lifted out a picture frame, beautifully carved of deep brown chestnut wood.

In the frame was a charcoal sketch of a woman sitting in a rocking-chair, holding a baby. The baby's arms were reaching up, touching the woman's face. The woman was looking down at the baby, smiling. Jonathan sat down in his rocking-chair and held the picture against his chest. He rocked slowly, his eyes closed. Two tears trailed into his beard.

When he finally took the picture to his workbench and began to carve, his fingers worked quickly and surely. He carved all through the night.

The next day, there was a knock on the widow McDowell's door.

When she opened it, there stood the wood-carver, his neck wrapped in a red scarf, holding a wooden box stuffed with straw.

"Mr Toomey!" said the widow. "What a surprise. Merry Christmas."

"The figures are ready," he said as he stepped inside.

From the box, Jonathan unpacked two curly sheep, happy sheep because they were with Jesus. He unpacked a proud cow and an angel, a very important angel with mighty wings stretching from its shoulders right down to the hem of its gown. He unpacked three Wise Men wearing their most wonderful robes, edged with fur and falling in rich folds.

He unpacked a serious and caring Joseph. He unpacked Mary wearing a rough woollen shawl, looking down, loving her precious baby son. Jesus was smiling and reaching up to touch his mother's face.

That day, Jonathan went to the Christmas service with the widow McDowell and Thomas. And that day in the churchyard the village children saw Jonathan throw back his head, showing his eyes as clear as an August sky, and laugh. No one ever called him Mr Gloomy again.

SUSAN WOJCIECHOWSKI

When I sat down to write *The Christmas Miracle of Jonathan Toomey* fifteen years ago, I had no idea of the marvellous and miraculous journey I was about to begin.

The idea came to me when I was a school librarian and felt the need to write a story that would illuminate what was for me the message of Christmas – hope. On that first Christmas a child was born who brought light and hope into a dark world. I decided to write about a child entering the life of a sorrowful man and bringing light and hope into that life.

From that point on, I have no memory of the actual plotting and writing of the story. There is no trace in my files of the mountains of rough, then edited, then re-edited longhand drafts that exist for all my other books. For *The Christmas Miracle of Jonathan Toomey* I have only a few pages of computer-printed text. I truly believe a power beyond me guided my hand. That same power may have been at work when one of the most gifted illustrators I can think of, P. J. Lynch, agreed to illustrate the story. The day I saw the first finished drawings, their power and beauty brought tears to my eyes.

Since the book's publication, I have met more wonderful book lovers than I can count. I've heard touching stories of their sharing the book with people in their lives who have needed its message of hope and healing.

For me, the most humbling and powerful reward of writing is that when someone reads my work I become connected to that person; I become a part of their lives even if just for a few moments. So thank you for choosing *The Christmas Miracle of Jonathan Toomey,* reading it, and giving me the honour of touching your life in some small way.

P. J. LYNCH

I knew from my first reading that *The Christmas Miracle of Jonathan Toomey* was a very special story. I had never read such a moving and beautifully paced text. At first, though, I doubted whether I was the right artist to illustrate it. But the more I reread it, the more I could visualize how the book might look, and the more I wanted to be the one who would create the pictures for it.

I set to – researching the settings, costumes and artefacts that would have been familiar to a wood-carver like Jonathan Toomey.

In my preparations, I went to greater lengths to achieve a sense of believability than I had done on any book before. However, the real challenge for me was to try to show what might be going on inside a character's head – or heart. If I have achieved that at all, it is in no small part due to the talents of the friends I asked to model for the main characters. They showed great patience with me and commitment to the project, and although I chose them for the particular way they looked, I was lucky that they turned out to be fine natural actors as well.

There was a good year of work in my paintings for the book, and a few nights when, like Toomey, I worked on into the early hours, until my eyelids drooped shut. I can't say whether my work on the book was inspired in the same mystical way that Susan's was, but it is true to say that as I painted, I had no doubts – and that is very unusual for me.

I will always be proud to have shared in the creation of *The Christmas Miracle of Jonathan Toomey.*

First published 1995 by Walker Books Ltd
87 Vauxhall Walk, London SE11 5HJ

This edition with CD published 2007

2 4 6 8 10 9 7 5 3 1

Text © 1995 Susan Wojciechowski

Illustrations © 1995 P.J. Lynch

The right of Susan Wojciechowski and P.J. Lynch to be
identified as author and illustrator respectively of this
work has been asserted by them in accordance with
the Copyright, Designs and Patents Act 1988

This book has been typeset in Columbus MT

Printed in China

British Library Cataloguing in Publication Data:
a catalogue record for this book is available
from the British Library

ISBN 978-1-4063-1040-5

www.walkerbooks.co.uk